For Adam -- Here's to this and many
more adventures to come. Thanks!

Library of Congress Control Number: 2016947440

ISBN 978-0-545-80429-5 (hardcover)
ISBN 978-0-545-80430-1 (paperback)

13 12 11 10   20 21 22 23
Printed in China   62

First edition, February 2017

Edited by Adam Rau
Book design by Phil Falco
Creative Director: David Saylor

2

3

4

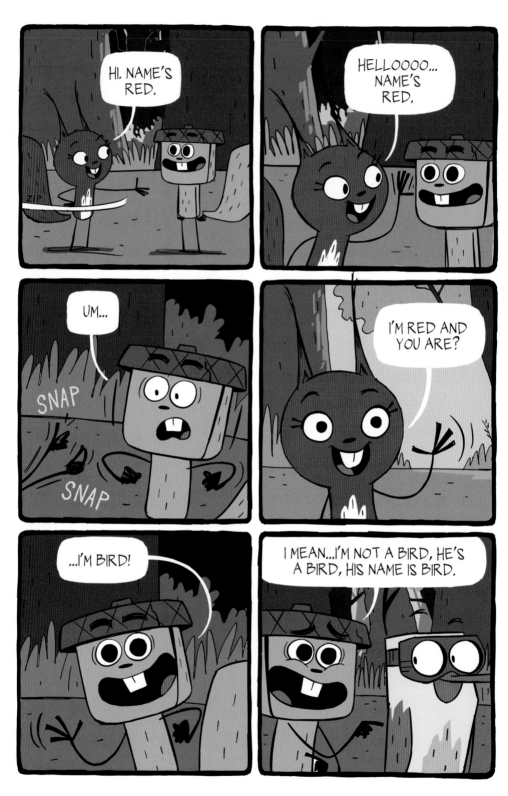

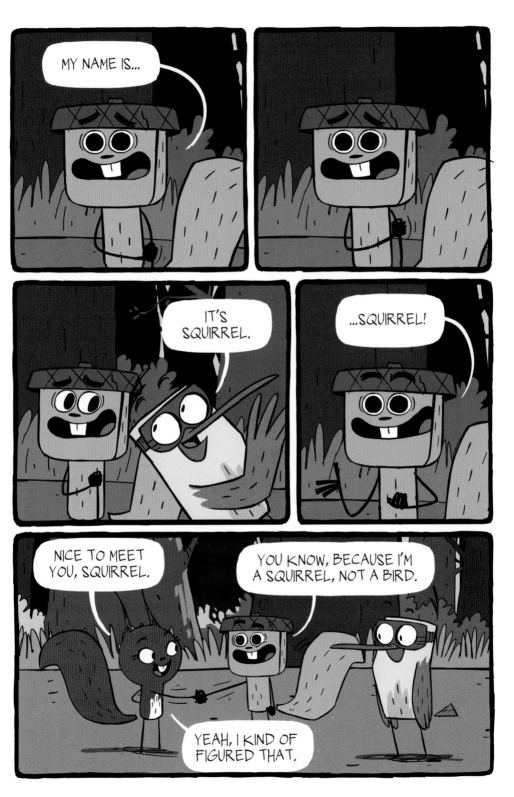

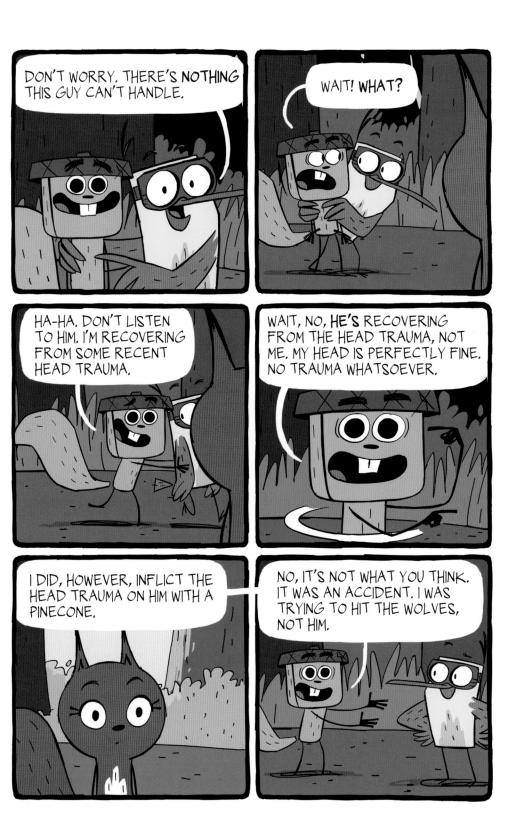

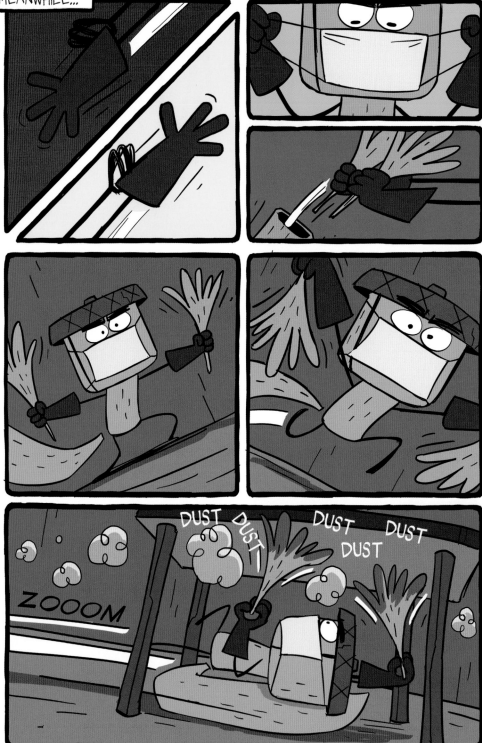

MEANWHILE...

DUST DUST DUST DUST DUST

ZOOOM

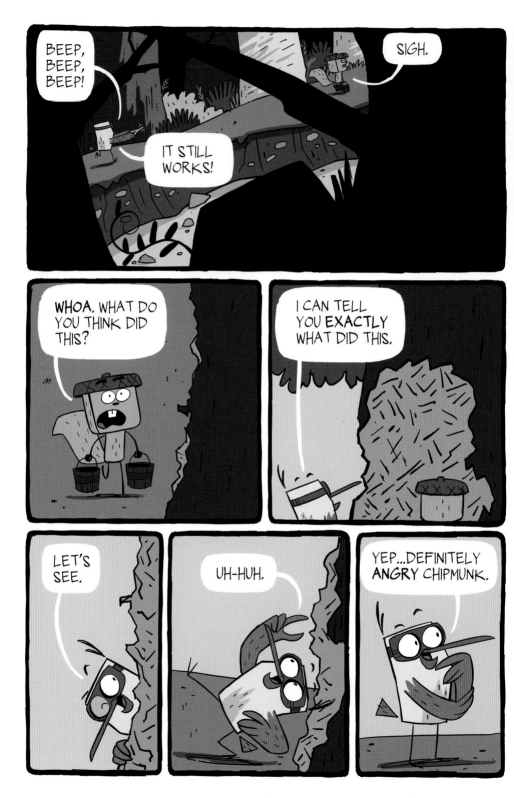

42

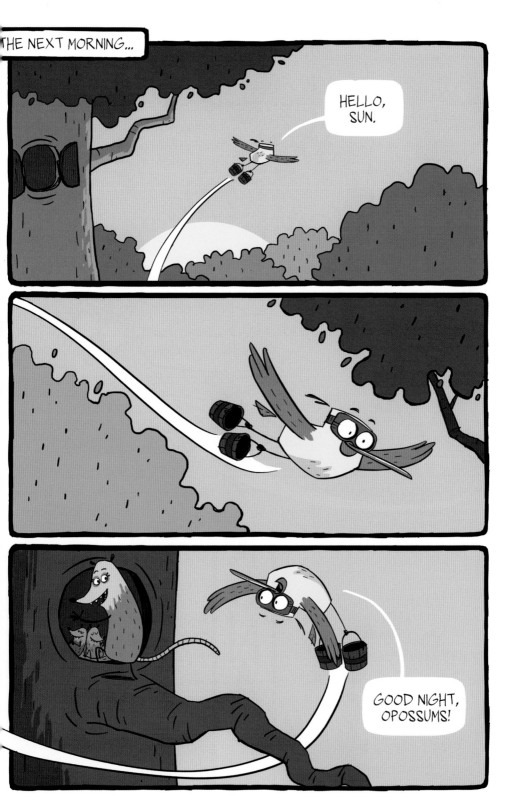

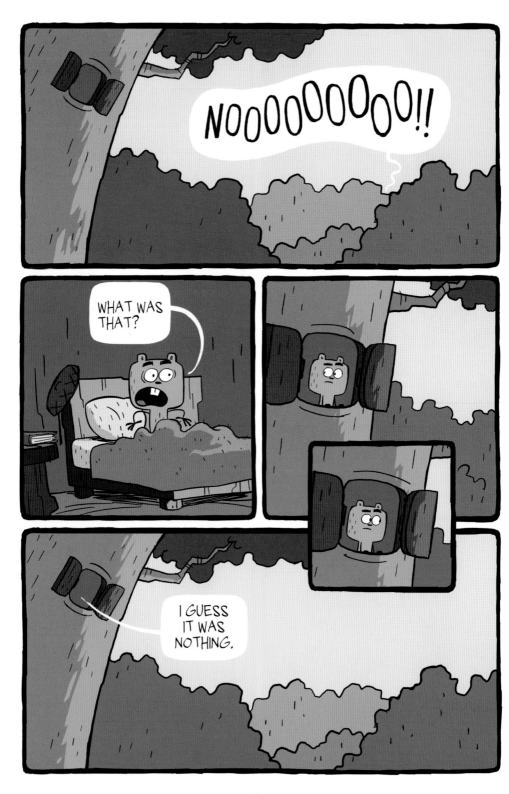

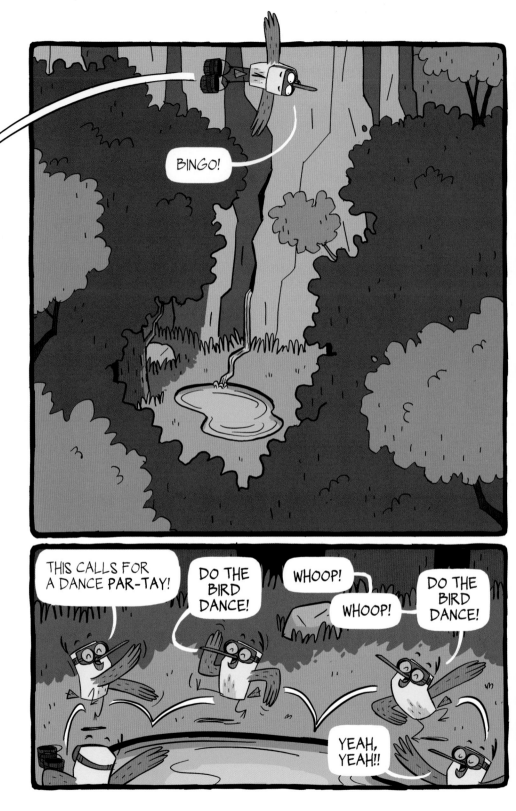

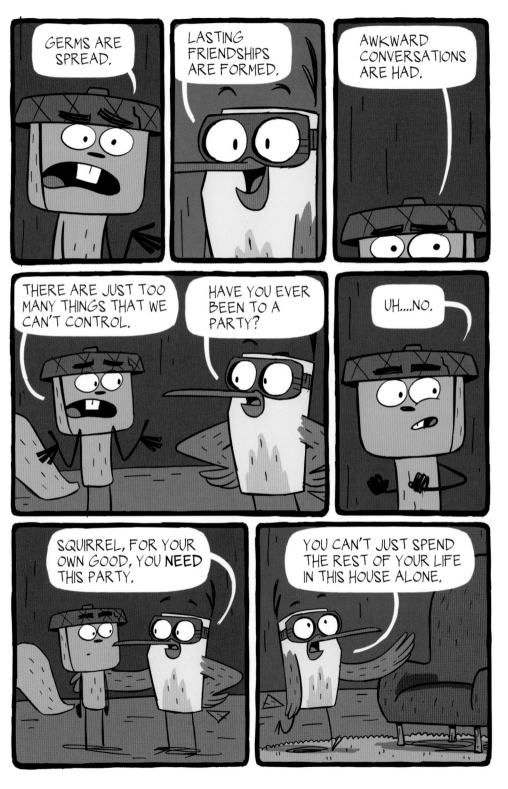

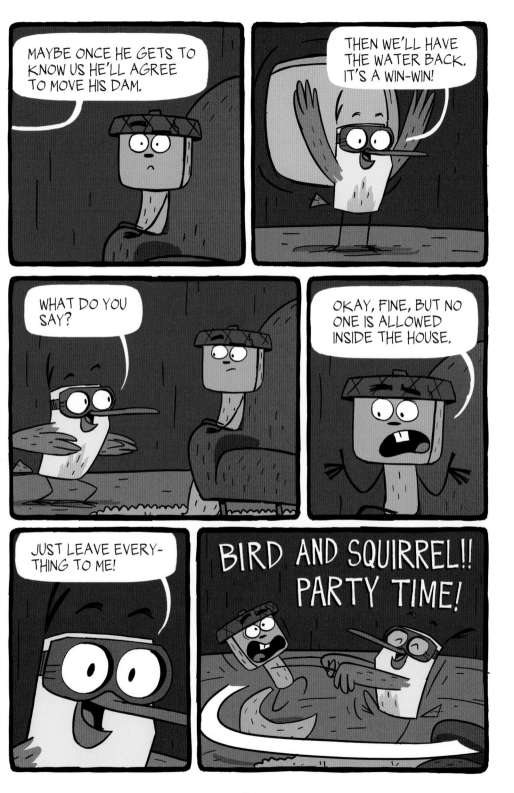

I THINK I KNOW A FASTER, SAFER WAY TO TRAVEL.

UP THERE?

YES. TREETOP TRAVEL IS THE SAFEST WAY TO GO.

WHOA!

HELP!

THAT LOOKS LIKE MOUSE'S HAT.

70

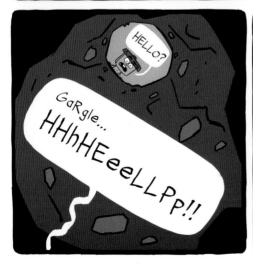

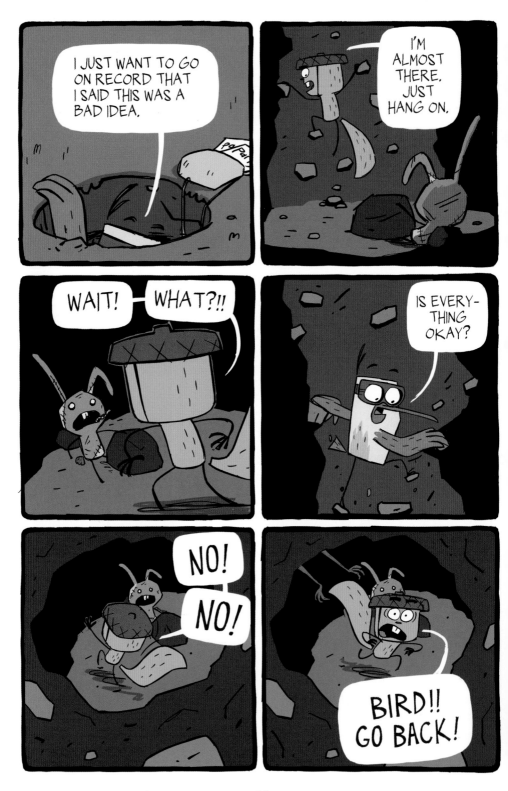

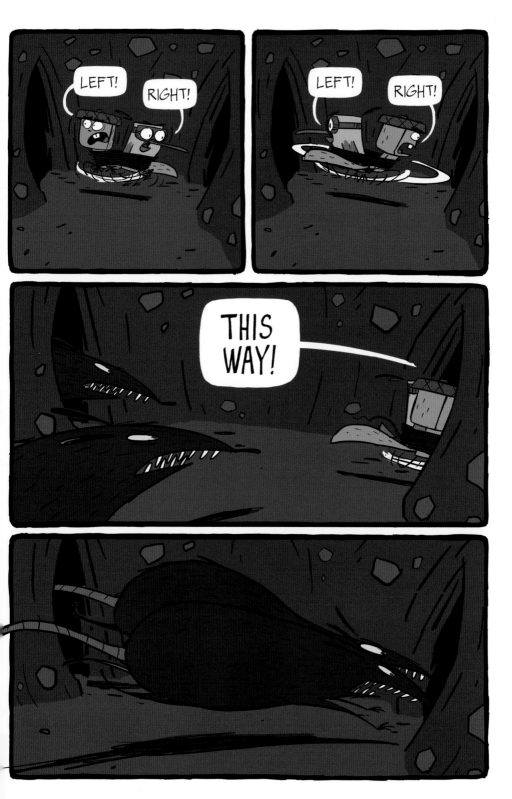

MMMM, SMELLS DELICIOUS. I WONDER WHAT'S FOR DINNER?

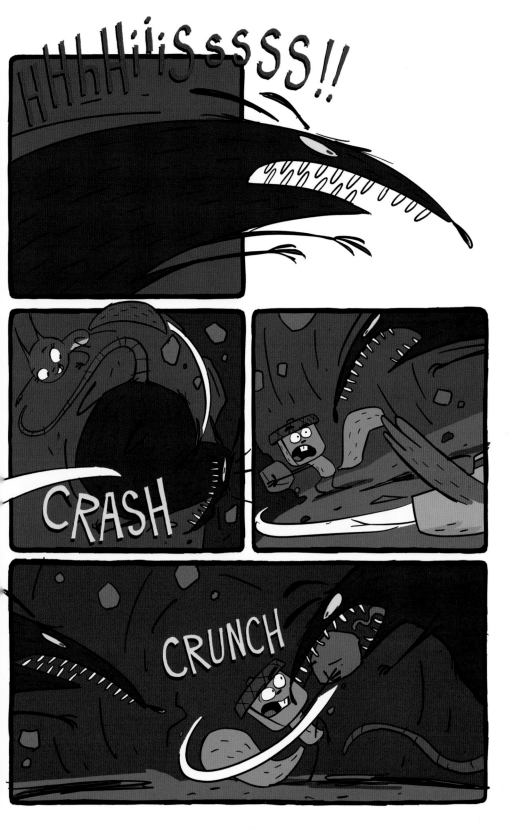

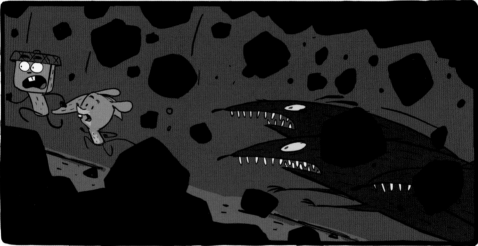

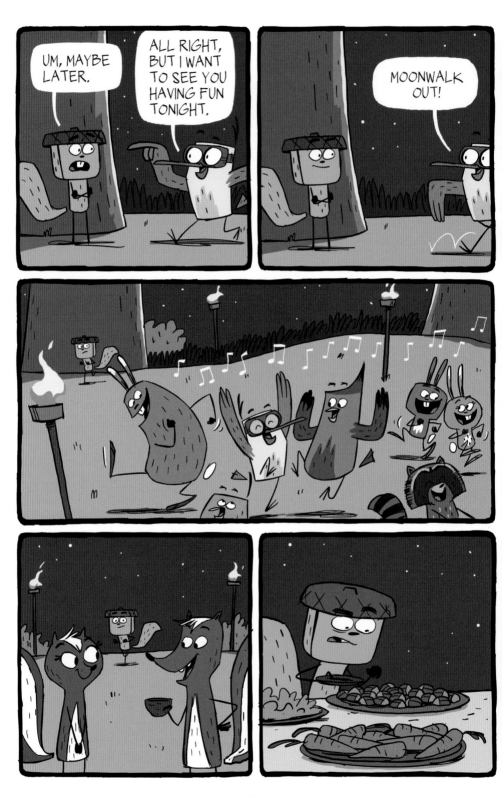

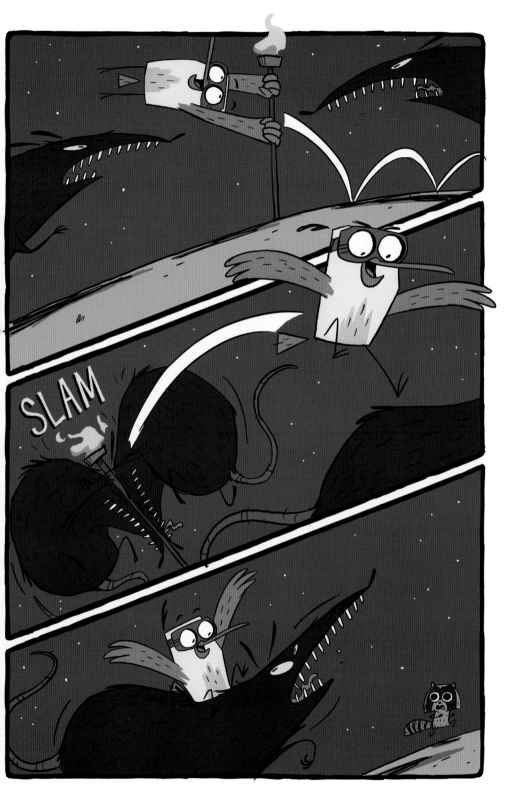

SLAM

137

143

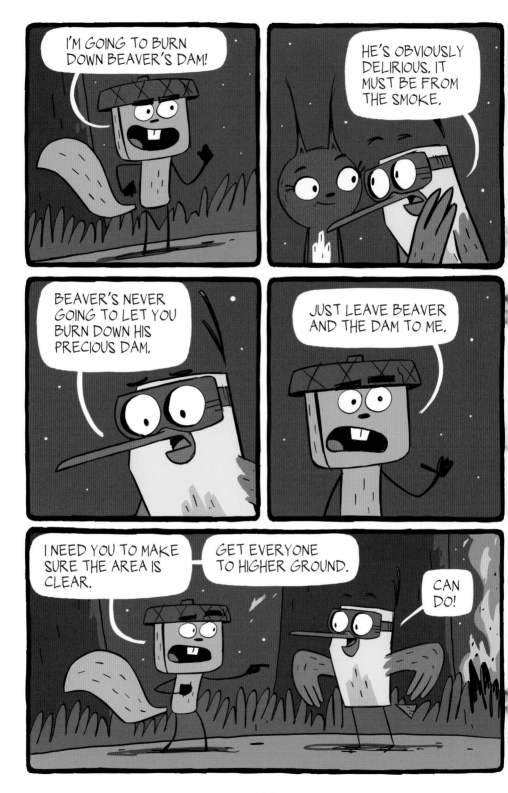

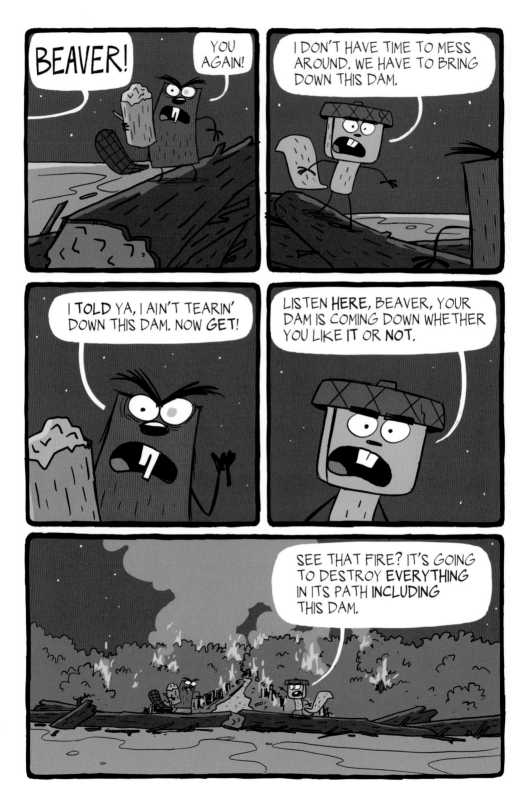

149

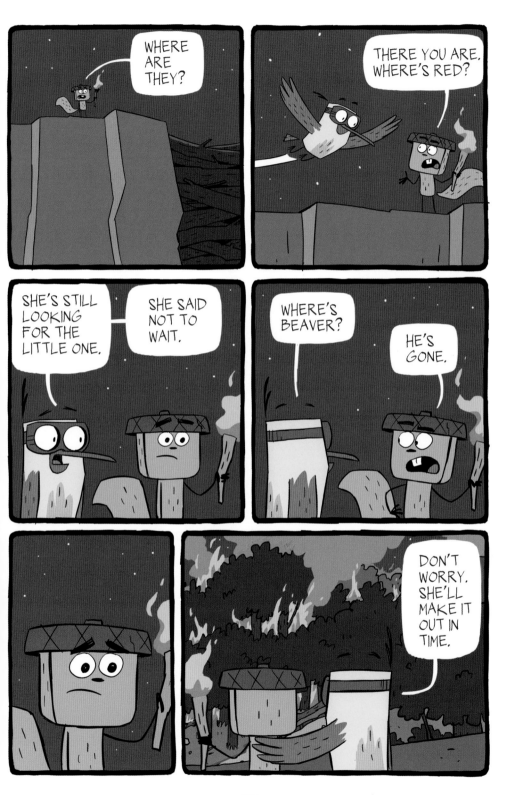

153

156

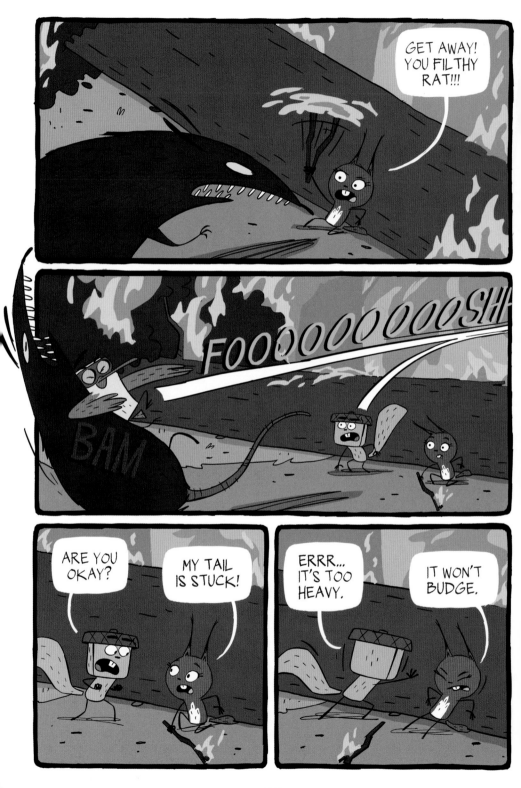

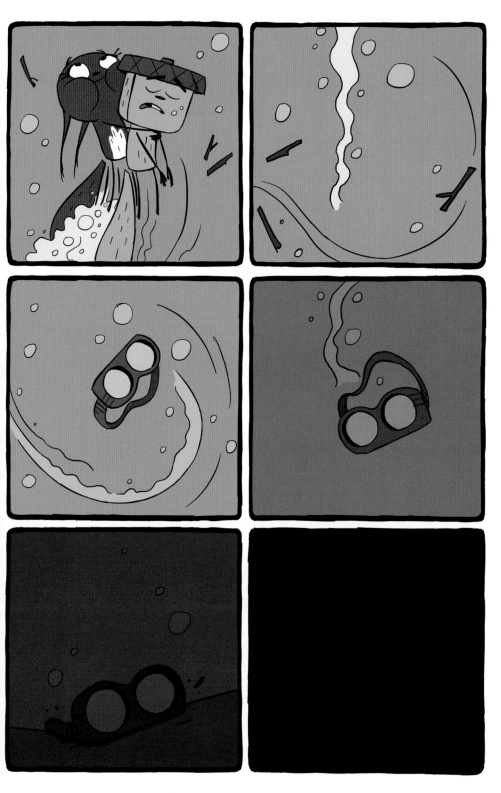

THREE SEASONS LATER...

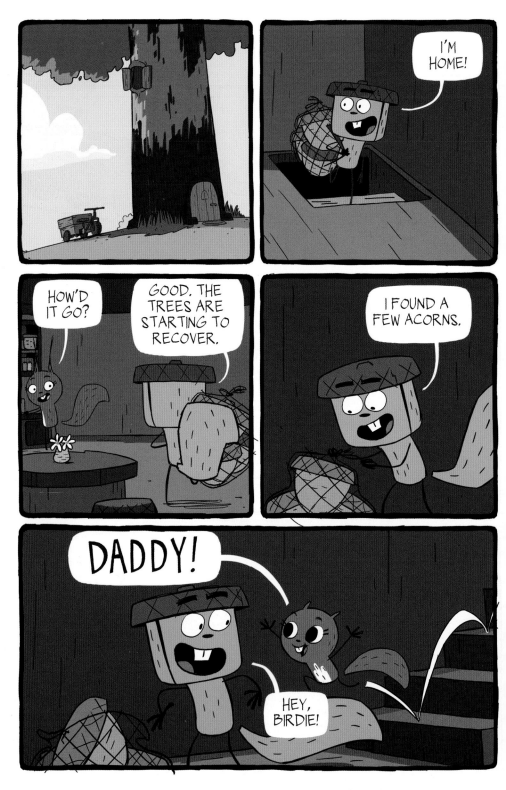